Caleb's Lighthouse

A 3 part Adventure of Courage,
Hope and Undying Love

Written by

Mark Kimball Moulton

Illustrated by

Stewart Sherwood

Other Books to Collect by
Storyteller Mark Kimball Moulton

• • •

A Snowman Named Just Bob
Everyday Angels
One Enchanted Evening
A Cricket's Carol
The Night at Humpback Bridge
Reindeer Moon

Text by Mark Kimball Moulton
Illustrations by Stewart Sherwood
© Copyright 2000
All Rights Reserved. Printed in the U.S.A.

Published by Lang Books
A Division of R. A. Lang Card Company, Ltd.
514 Wells Street • Delafield, WI 53018
262.646.2211 • www.lang.com

ISBN: 0-7412-0736-2

10 9 8 7 6 5 4 3 2 1
Second Edition

Presented to _____

on this Date _____

From _____

To my Mother.

Stewart

• • •

This story was inspired by the
magical spirit of Loreena McKennitt,
and dedicated to
my wonderful family and friends...
most especially Karen and Lane,
and my Godchildren, Melissa, Alecia,
Conor, and of course, Sean.

Mark

Part One

The sea breaks wild and stormy,
waves crash upon the shore—
then roll back in upon themselves
to pound the shore once more.

A fiendish storm with pelting rain
blows in with gale-wind force.
As lightning crackles through the air,
thunder bellows its remorse.

It seems as if Neptune, himself,
has risen from the sea,
to throw his mighty fury 'round
and cause this storm to be.

Yet, heedless of this fury,
out of the fog he does appear,
like a ghostly apparition
of the pirate, old Bluebeard.

But it is only dear, good Caleb,
ever faithful in his search.
Each night he comes and looks to sea
from his rocky, windswept perch.

His oilskin coat slaps in the wind,
white hair and beard soaked through.
He holds his ancient lantern high,
his cap is blown askew.

And though his years are many,
his eyes are clear and keen–
the one assent he offers age
is the staff on which he leans.

The rain pours down in brittle sheets
washing o'er his weathered face,
joining with his salty tears
that fall with no disgrace.

And just behind dear Caleb
stands the lighthouse, brave and true,
sending out its guiding light
to lost souls all night through.

As each beam from the lighthouse
turns 'round and 'round again,
Caleb finds his thoughts return
to where he once had been.

For many, many years ago,
he had the perfect life.
No man had been a richer one,
with home and child and wife.

You see, Caleb had been a fisherman
as his family was before –
a tough, demanding, lonely job,
but an honest one, for sure.

He grew up on the ocean,
was taught from his first day
that, with respect, the sea will give
a good life, come what may.

As a young man, he was fearless,
strong and brave and true,
with coal black hair and calloused hands
and piercing eyes of blue.

He'd laugh at wicked weather,
and cast off every morn,
returning with a full day's catch,
whether sun or fog or storm.

But years
soon passed
and it was time
for him to settle down.
He packed his bags
and bid goodbye
and headed for the town.

He'd never leave the ocean,
nor forsake his way of life.
He simply took a
well-earned break
to find himself a wife.

The day was warm and sunny,
he remembered it so well—
when first he saw Loreena,
and deep in love he fell.

She was strolling through the village,
a basket in her hand.
He knew then that no fairer lass
could be found throughout the land!

She turned by chance and stumbled,
Caleb caught her 'fore she fell.
It took but one mere second,
and she was under Caleb's spell.

It was clear to her
he was the one
she had longed for all her days –
with his dark, good looks
and dashing style
and gentle, caring ways.

Sweet Loreena was the miller's girl
'till she was Caleb's bride.
From that day on she worked with him
and never left his side.

Trained in the ways of city life,
the sea was a mystery.
But Loreena determined early on
to work as hard as he.

She learned of tides and currents,
of cod, and blues, and whales.
She mended nets and tied true knots
and even learned to sail.

They built a good and sturdy home
of stone and brick and wood.
They watched the seagulls circle
from the cliff on which it stood.

Each night he'd come from fishing,
she'd greet him at the door.
His eyes would tear from happiness—
no man could want for more.

She'd say...

"Caleb, love, I do confess,
I really don't know how
I lived before without your love.
I treasure my life now."

He'd say...

"My heart is like that lighthouse,
with its signal, strong and true.
Should you need strength or comfort,
I'll always be there for you."

For several years they flourished–
time treated them with love.
Soon life would grant another gift,
a blessing from above.

That spring, as days grew warm and rich,
and the world blossomed with joy,
Loreena gave Caleb a child,
a bouncing baby boy.

Sean was the name they gave their son,
after Caleb's father's dad–
a handsome boy with eyes like hers
and hair like Caleb had.

Now when Caleb left for sea,
two loves he'd kiss at dawn–
his beauty, sweet Loreena,
and his world...
their new son, Sean.

Part Two

But soon, as fate would have it,
one day while Caleb sailed,
the sky grew dark and stormy
and the wind began to wail.

Loreena, with her son held close,
paced from room to room.
A little nagging voice inside
warned of impending doom.

Rarely did she worry,
for Caleb knew the sea.
He'd return to her before a storm
would ever come to be.

But this day there was something
that bothered her, no end.
She tried to keep fair busy
with household duties to attend.

Caleb looked into the sky,
felt the wind shift north to east—
white caps rose around his ship,
the threat of storm increased.

It was too much for Loreena
to sit inside and wait.
She threw down her old mending,
ran through the garden gate—

to the cliff over the ocean,
she took up vigil there—
fell to her knees, she closed her eyes,
sent up a silent prayer.

Waves pounded at good Caleb's ship,
groans echoed from the mast—
never in all his sailing days
had a storm come up so fast!

The sky grew dark, the east wind howled,
her hair whipped 'round her face—
she clutched her shawl about her chest,
and again began to pace.

Caleb headed straight for shore,
tried to outrun the gale –
but from nowhere came a cyclone blast
that tore apart the sail!

By now Loreena's nerves were taut,
this was far too much to bear –
"Cal-e-e-e-b," she screamed out o'er the ledge,
but it was lost throughout the air.

Caleb strained against the ropes,
waves smashed about the deck –
then, just for one brief second,
he felt a shiver down his neck.

For as the storm was thrashing
and he battled to and fro,
he was sure he heard Loreena
calling deep inside his soul...

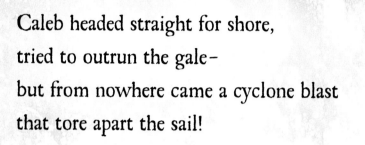

She ran back to the cottage
and grabbed a woolen coat,
wrapped Sean in warm, dry blankets,
and headed for her boat.

She placed Sean safely in the bottom,
untied them from the moor,
and as the boat began to thrash,
felt a shiver at her core–

And as clear as day was Caleb's face
before her in the sky.
She was certain, too, she heard him call
to her, from deep inside.

"Lor-e-e-e-na," screamed good Caleb,
as lightning struck the ship!
Timbers cracked and splinters flew—
the mast began to tip.

He was thrown into the churning sea—
he coughed and gasped for air.
He watched his ship be split apart—
his heart broke in despair.

He flailed his arms to stay afloat,
the wreckage spiraling past—
he grabbed a severed timber,
and held on to it fast.

The waves smashed down upon him,
and spun him 'round and 'round.
He lost all sense of direction,
and still the sea did pound.

She fought the waves with all her might—
she did her very best,
but the storm had gathered its full strength—
she was no match for the test.

Splinters ripped Loreena's hands
as the oars were torn away.
The tiny boat spun 'round and 'round,
and was dragged far out of the bay.

She knew what she'd done was foolish,
to risk her son, her life—
but at the time, she had to try,
for she was Caleb's Wife!

Now all that fate had left for her
was to fight just to survive—
and with every ounce of courage,
she'd keep them both alive!

She lay down next to her good son,
pulled a tarp over them both,
held him close and closed her eyes,
and then she made this oath:

"No matter what should happen,
how hard I have to cope –
by all the power within my soul,
I'll never give up hope!"

Caleb's strength was slowly ebbing,
his muscles ached with strain.
He didn't know just where he was,
could barely stand the pain.

Then he thought of sweet Loreena
and his newborn baby, Sean,
and the promise that he made to them
gave him strength to carry on.

Almost like a miracle,
he saw the faintest gleam,
and from far off in the distance
Caleb saw the beam!

He splashed and swam and paddled
toward the lighthouse on the bluff.
Love gave him hope and courage,
though the seas were still so rough.

The surf threw him on the shoreline –
he crawled up on his knees.
He stumbled toward salvation –
   his love, his home, his peace.

A salty tear fell from his eye
when their cottage came to view.
He ran down the path, threw back the door –
    in his soul, a cold wind blew...

He called out to Loreena.
He ran from room to room.
He saw his son's cold, empty crib
and felt a dreaded doom.

Icy fingers grabbed him
and traveled down his spine.
He stood dead still and this he heard
float softly through his mind...

    "No matter what should happen,
    how hard I have to cope –
    by all the power within my soul,
    I'll never give up hope."

He knew then what had happened,
with every fiber of his life –
that Loreena had tried to save him,
for she was Caleb's Wife.

One day just blew into the next
as they drifted on and on.
No sign of land was visible
to Loreena and her son, Sean.

And as darkness overcame her,
she heard these words float through–
   "My heart is like that lighthouse,
   I'll always be there for you."

for-e-e-e-na... S-e-a-a-a-n...

He ran blindly to the cliff's edge,
roared out his pain and grief–
his body racked with bitter sobs,
that brought him no relief.

The mist fell...wet...and heavy,
a thick fog came spiraling in.
Heaven wept unanswered tears,
thunder softened to a din...

Part Three

The sea breaks calm and quiet...
moonlight peaks between the clouds
and dances on the rippled waves,
as the ocean settles down.

To him it seems like yesterday,
though years have come and gone,
since that tragic day when Caleb lost
Loreena and their son, Sean.

Now good Caleb is an old man,
and more and more he finds
his thoughts returning to the past,
and those dreams of days gone by.

He'd no idea how long he stood,
shook his head to clear the past.
Sometime when he was lost in thought,
the storm had said its last.

A bitter chill began to seep
into his old and weary bones,
and just like every other night,
it was time to head for home.

But somehow, this night was different–
he knew it deep inside–
and just like it happened once before,
a shiver ran down his spine.

Caleb felt someone behind him –
just who, he couldn't tell.
He stumbled as he turned around,
was caught before he fell.

He looked to his benefactor,
uttered a startled cry –
there stood a man with coal black hair
and sweet Loreena's eyes.

Tears streamed down old Caleb's face
for this man was his own boy!
But now the tears that Caleb shed
were not of pain, but joy!

"but... How?"

was all Caleb could say,
he could manage nothing more.
And here's what Sean did tell Caleb
on that rocky, windswept shore:

"I was just a tiny babe
when that storm took Mother and me.
But she recalled the day so well
it's fixed in my memory.

It was love that set her course that day,
her love for you and me.
That deep, abiding, reverent love
one has for family.

And though that storm had bested her,
it never shook her faith.
She always said that, come what may,
she'd fight to keep us safe.

And one day reunite us,
husband, wife and son.
Even as she breathed her last,
she knew that day would come.

For days and weeks we drifted –
the wind captained our boat,
then tossed us on an island
that was unknown and remote...

A cold, mist-shrouded island...but we made a good life there,
as seals watched us from the rocky cliffs, and seabirds circled in the air.

We discovered an old homestead, long-deserted, lost in time.
Took shelter in the stony croft. Took our meals from the brine.

But never did she give up hope,
whatever came to be.
I'd find her on the shore
each dawn...
just staring
out to sea.

And as the stars came out each night,
she'd teach me North from West –
then sing to me this lullaby
when she lay me down to rest –

'You must look for the lighthouse,
its beam is strong and true.
That's where you'll find your father –
he'll be waiting there for you.'

Mother lived her life with fortitude,
with dignity and grace –
and though she missed you desperately,
of regret, she had no trace.

For she taught me not to waste life,
that each day's a precious jewel.
But the days that Mother treasured most
were the days we spent with you.

The last thought that she shared with me
is that true love has no end,
and that she would wait there for us
beyond the rainbow's bend.

Soon after...
I began my search to reunite myself with you—
and though so many years have passed,

I know Mother's with us too."

Epilogue

Sean settled in with Caleb
and made his life upon the sea—
found true love with a local girl
and raised a family.

Caleb took great pleasure,
with a grandchild on each knee,
in recalling tales of yesteryear
and of his days upon the sea.

Still, to this day good Caleb waits,
though now contentment fills his eyes,
for he knows Loreena waits for him...

...beyond the rainbow sky.